Just One Flick of a Finger

By Marybeth Lorbiecki

Illustrated by David Diaz

Just One Flick of a Finger

Dial Books • New York

Published by Dial Books
A Division of Penguin Books USA Inc.
375 Hudson Street
New York, New York 10014

Library of Congress Cataloging in Publication Data

Lorbiecki, Marybeth.
Just one flick of a finger / by Marybeth Lorbiecki; illustrated by David Diaz.—1st ed.
p.   cm.
Summary: A young boy takes a gun to school to scare off the bully who has been
tormenting him, and the gun is accidentally fired during a scuffle.
ISBN 0-8037-1948-5 (trade)—ISBN 0-8037-1949-3 (lib. bdg.)
[1.Firearms—Fiction. 2.Bullies—Fiction. 3.Stories in rhyme.] I.Diaz, David, ill. II.Title.
PZ8.3.L865Ju 1996 [E]—dc20 95-23491 CIP AC

To all those kids who live in fear or awe of guns, that we might make their lives safer
and more filled with love, hope, and mentoring.

Special thanks to teachers Muriel Dubois and Jane O. Soltau
and their classes for being such discerning readers and willing,
friendly critics. And to agent Edythea Ginis Selman and editor Diane Arico
for making this possible. And also to Mom and Jean for their help.
—MbL

For Jericho,
Sweet Fragrance of My Life.
—DD

Hey you,
you cool?
Then I've got
a story for you.

The rule
at my school
is you're a fool
if you can't get
your hand on a gun.

So my friend Sherms and me,
we stuck together
like a pair of Reeboks
and tried to stay
out of everyone's way.

Couldn't be done.

Reebo had it in for me.
He was mean as a needle
and thin as a weenie.

One day in May
before the first bell rang,
Reebo was in my face,
calling me "Fat Jack"
and "White Rat."

Sherms, who has muscles
where I have Twinkies,
edged between us.

Reebo took a step back.
His right hand flashed
toward his pocket,
and we both froze.

Before our breath could melt,
Ms. Johnson yelled,
"What're you boys doing?"

Reebo just smiled,
like ice sliced thin,
and we backed away.

After that,
Sherms and I
made a blood brothers' pact
to stick together.

Still, I got to thinking how
I'd like a gun—
to be swift as lightning
and hot as a racing engine.
I wanted to be bad,
so bad no one would mess with me,
especially not Reebo.

I knew the trick—
just one flick
of a finger
on a trigger,
and Reebo would be off my case.

The cost was high—
I had to be sly
to sneak that gun
from my dad.
He kept it in a box,
but I could trip the lock.

So I stole Dad's revolver
from its place in the drawer
as he slept off his latest beer.
I wondered then and there
if he would care
if something happened to me.
But then I let it be.

My thoughts turned to steel
at the feel
of the cold metal
and the black grip.

The weight of it,
swinging 'round in my pocket,
hit me in the ribs
like a big heartbeat.

I snuck it to the bathroom
to practice drawing it
fast, sleek, and slick,
like a cowboy or a TV cop.

Next day at school
I flashed the gun to Sherms
and he freaked.
"You crazy, man?"
he shouted.
"You think you're so big,
so fine?
Know what happened
to my big bro?
Lee thought he was
top of the heap too.
Got a gun to PROTECT himself,
and what'd he do?
Fought with his girl
and lost his head.
Now he's doing time
without a dime,
and his love took off
after all that blood."

What could I say?
"Coward!" Sherms muttered,
"I thought you were somebody."
Then he walked away.

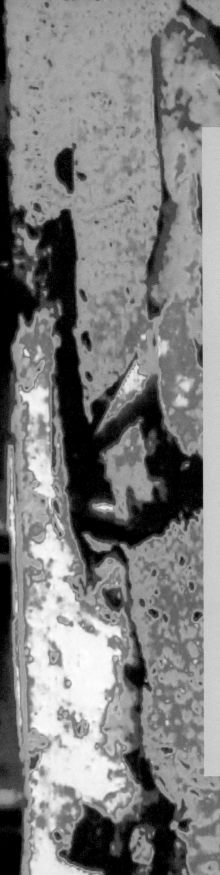
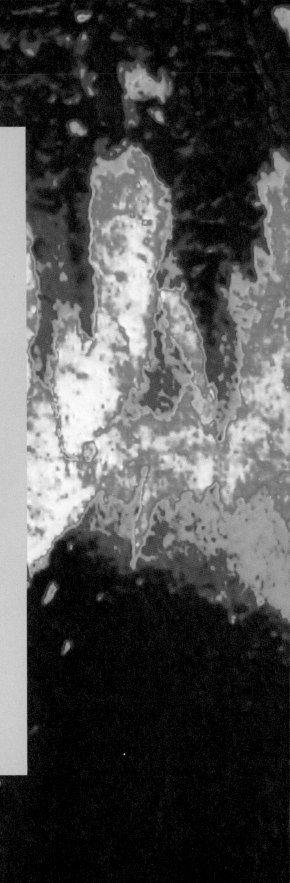

I closed my eyes,
and chucked at the nearest tree.

Reebo came slinking over,
his hands deep in his jacket.

"Fatty Boy loses his lunch,"
he hollered,
and everyone turned to stare.
Shame burned my fingers
to the icy metal.

"Say it again, Reebo,
and I'll lose it on you."
I can't believe
I said it,
but I did
and then leaned forward,
tipping the gun
out of my pocket
so he could see it.

A voice screamed, "DON'T !!!"
and I was tackled from in front.
As I hit the pavement,
I heard the gun go off.

When I woke,
my head was mummy wrapped
and heavy as a bowling ball.
Sherms was in the bed next to me,
with a mask over his face.
They said he'd been
shot in the lungs and
had lost lots of blood.

I felt froze,
cold to the bone—
my brother, my only friend,
had come to this end
'cause of me,
me and that killing machine.

But thanks over and over
to the doctors and God—
Sherms made it.

Now we're really blood brothers
'cause I begged to share,
and they let me give him
the blood I could spare.

And there's one thing more.
His brother Lee came home
on the big parole
with one glass eye
and a twisted nose.
He told us that
in the old ice house
he got a dive into
the meanest, ugliest hell alive,
where most don't survive—
they just shrivel up inside
and die.
And Lee says he wants
to keep Sherms and I
"straight as a church steeple
and proud as a Masai."
He got smart in the pen
about drugs and guns,
and electricity.

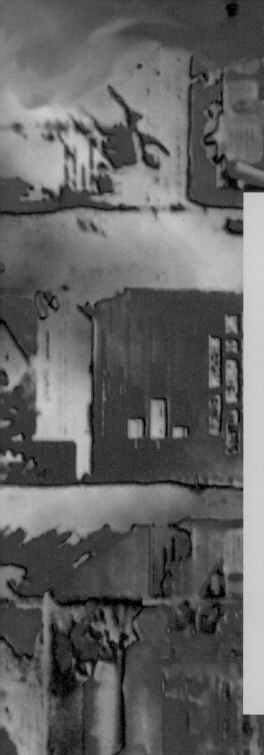

So instead of shooting up,
he's wiring up
in a business
of his own.
Sherms and I
will be at his side—
once I've paid the cost
of the respect I've lost
and the laws
that I shot through.

So the cool
can drool
for all I care.
I got two bros in the know
and lightning in my mind.

The paintings in this book were created with acrylics, watercolor,
and gouache on Arches watercolor paper.
The backgrounds were composed and photographed by the illustrator
and digitally manipulated by Jericho Diaz.
The title and text type was set in Gabrielle,
a font created by the illustrator.
Designed by David Diaz with special assistance from Troy Viss.